# The King
# Of
# The Things

## As told by
## Adrian
## Beckingham

MOGZILLA

First published by Mogzilla in 2013.
This edition 2014.


ISBN: 978-1-906132-50-7 PAPERBACK


Text copyright: Adrian Beckingham.
Cover by Jason Smith. www.macaruba.com.
Cover ©Mogzilla 2013.

www.mogzilla.co.uk

# WARNING!

This story is an ADULT FREE ZONE. Why? Because it is simply too scary, or too horridly disgusting, for most adults. We know this is true. Kids can handle it. Usually. Adults can't. Mostly. There are very few grown who can sit through the full telling of this tale. Not without scrunching up their noses, or scrinching up their eyes, or gasping "EEEwwwww" or just saying "Yuk that's disgusting" before the tale reaches its end. Very brave grown-ups may be allowed to stay, if at least one child will vouch that they can handle it.

So now you know *that*, we can carry on.

# Chapter 1
# Tax and Hunch

This story happened once upon a time in a small village not so far away. The village was surrounded by fields, and the fields were surrounded by forests. There was a wide river running alongside the village and a small stone bridge leading to the fields beyond.

Ooops! And I have already made one mistake in my telling of this tale. It's true to say that the fields used to be surrounded by forest, but by the time this tale took place, some of the trees had begun to disappear.

For in the village lived a young man named Tax. Tax had been born lucky. He was the most handsome baby that any parents could ask for. When he began school he was the tallest boy in his class, and the fastest, and the best at playing ball games. He told the funniest jokes, laughed the loudest, was the most popular dancer. Soon his friends began to call him 'Tax the Terrific!' and always cheered him on at absolutely everything. Tax loved village life, mainly because there was nobody better at anything than he was. He was the best at swimming, the best at climbing the hills, and the bravest when it came to entering the forest – although he never dared to go too far. For it was said that terrible frightening things that cannot be described lived deep in that mysterious wood.

In the same village lived a young man whose friends called him – well nothing actually. This was because he had no friends, unless you can count the squirrels, whom he often fed by hand. Some said he was the most unfortunate person living in the village. You see, when he was born, he had a tiny lump the size of a pea jutting out right there on his shoulder. And as he grew that pea of flesh and blood and bone grew too. Life had never been easy for him. Things had gone well enough at first. He had a handsome face and was born to a caring mother and father who lived in a tiny two-room cottage that nestled near the bridge on the outskirts of the village. Each night as he lay below his quilt, the gentle lullaby of the river just outside his window helped him smile, and he often carried that smile into his dreams.

But of course as he grew, and that lump grew too, people started to notice. By the time he began at the village school that pea-sized lump on his shoulder was more the size of a golf ball. Soon it had grown so much it was almost the size of a second head, though one with no eyes, or ears, or hair, or brain – just a lump of bone and gristle covered by flesh.

It was because of this lump that everyone in the village called him 'Hunch', which is short for 'hunchback'. For indeed, although that name is not used these days (because it sounds cruel to our modern ears), alas, a 'hunchback' is exactly what he was. That hunch grew so heavy that it felt like a mountain. Its grip on his shoulder and upper back kept him leaning forward in a stoop. From an early age, Hunch carried a staff of twisted hazel cut from a tree that had fallen onto the forest floor, which his father gave him to use as a walking stick.

# Chapter 2
# Cruel School

When it was time for games in the schoolyard, Hunch didn't do too well. He could neither run nor catch nor throw terribly well. The hump kept him off balance. He could not swim so well as the others. Or climb. And when the village held a dance, the other children would sneer and snigger at Hunch's awkward lumbering. There was so much laughter when Hunch tried to join in, that he soon held himself back.

One day Tax thought up a new name for Hunch. Tax thought the name was a stroke of genius. And judging by the laughter of the other children, it seemed as if everyone thought so too. Soon all the children began to call him 'Hunch the Horrid' or just 'Horrid Hunch' for short. And he knew why. He was hopeless at games, and useless at sports, and no good at anything. Hunch the Horrid seemed to stick. But nobody hated that hump more than he did. When the other children mocked him and laughed and jeered and said how stupid he was – I'm afraid to say that 'Horrid Hunch' believed them.

If Hunch was a loser in every way, Terrific Tax, on the other hand, was a ring-leader. And one of the ways Tax liked to take the lead was in bullying. Tax was King of the thugs, you might say. He especially liked targeting Hunch, who had no friends to defend him. Tax would point at Hunch with a grin and tell him to swim, or to climb, or to dance. Just because he knew Hunch couldn't do it. He would flick twigs or stones into Hunch's hair, or threaten to throw him in the river.

Hunch soon learnt to spend his time away from other children, for they were always mocking him for how different he was. He would go to school unhappily every day, wondering what bullying lay in store for him. Hunch lived for the freedom of the afternoons, which he spent walking with the aid of his twisted hazel staff, exploring the edge of the forest. Sometimes he'd sit on the riverbank with a line cast into the water, catching fish. Hunch used to love carrying them home for his father to cook over the open fire.

It was during one of those quiet moments fishing on the riverbank that he first made friends with the wild squirrels who lived in the forest.

He would watch those squirrels leap and bound along the high branches, and as they grew used to him, they would move closer, coming down the trunks carefully towards him.

One afternoon he had some sandwiches he hadn't eaten at school in his pocket. He had gone to a tall tree with wide majestic branches. It sat at the end of a wide corridor of trees, overlooking the river, in a place nobody else seemed to go. Someone had long ago rolled a circle of smooth stones around that tree, and Hunch found them perfect for sitting on and listening to the birds, or watching the flow of the nearby river. He unwrapped his sandwiches and broke off a few crumbs. He threw them out a little so that the squirrels did not have to come closer than they dared to nibble them. Then all of a sudden, the squirrel with the bushiest tale leapt straight down from a tree onto Hunch's shoulder. He gave a yelp of alarm and then he laughed. He named this squirrel Quiz, because he thought it was such a puzzle that a squirrel seemed so relaxed around him. Nobody else was. People saw a hunchback, not the boy inside.

This beautiful tree so full of life within the circle of stone stools became Hunch's favourite hideaway after that. He named the place Quiz's

Tree. Hunch thought this squirrel Quiz was so beautiful. She had the brightest eyes, and the shiniest red fur, with a lovely white patch right down her front. Hunch soon learned that unlike him, she was a bit of a ring-leader. With Quiz leading the pack, Hunch soon had every one of those wild squirrels feeding tamely from his hand. From then on they were always his friends. It did not seem to matter what part of the riverbank Hunch sat on, Quiz's little dray of squirrels would find him. He was so grateful for the way these furry friends would jump straight up onto his lap. Quiz soon made Hunch's humped shoulder her favourite perch. She would sit on Hunch's hunched back and clean her fur and paws, sniffing the cool air.

Sometimes a large bird of prey or a fox might be seen. Quiz would take fright and leap off with her dray of squirrel friends running behind her. Those squirrels would scamper away and clamber into the safety of the nearby trees. They danced and hopped about in those uppermost branches, way up high in the canopy, and often Hunch lost sight of them as they headed deeper into the trees. Sometimes he was sure Quiz was trying to call him up there, to run with them across the roof of the forest. How Hunch wished he could leap among those branches with them, and disappear into the woods. But his hump stopped him climbing. And like all the other children, Hunch knew not to venture too far into the forest. His parents had always warned him that strange unimaginable things lived in there. Picking on Hunch was one of Tax's favourite things, but at least Hunch could escape into the quietness of the forest.

********

One afternoon, Tax's grandfather taught the lad how to chop wood with an axe. From then on, Tax was often found skirting along the edge of the trees with his axe at the ready. Tax loved chopping trees. It made him feel very grown up, fearless and strong. As you know he never dared enter too far lest some terrifying unmentionable thing should leap out and grab him.

"I'm a grown up now. I am a woodsman," the youthful Tax would tell his friends. He insisted they called him 'Tax The Axe.' A name he had made up with another stroke of genius. Soon Tax had cut down more trees than anyone else in the village. The edge of the forest was slowly but surely creeping ever further away.

Playing at being the woodcutter, Tax would sometimes wake before dawn and head out to the edge of the forest. He could stand there for hours cutting down trees all alone. The trees shook and trembled silently under his swinging blade. Hunch heard some of the adults speaking among themselves, saying Tax had an anger in him he was trying to let out. Hunch knew one thing for sure. Tax had always been lucky, but he made others feel bad. In all those slow hours spent alone, as the sap of the trees dripped like sticky honey from the wounds and scars he'd made, never once did the young woodcutter feel any sadness about the trees he'd damaged.

One afternoon as Tax walked to the edges of the forest, he saw Hunch stooped over on his knees on the ground. Tax stopped and stooped and watched to see what Hunch was up to. The hunchback seemed to be patting the ground, but Tax could not see past Hunch's bobbing frame. Then Hunch stood up. In a patch of freshly dug earth, stood a tiny sapling.

Tax roared with laughter, simply because he felt he must make fun of everything that Hunch did. He always had. He always would. Why stop now? The woodcutter strode up to the hunchback and said, "What are you doing, Horrid?"

Hunch groaned. Why was Tax always

hanging around the edge of the forest these days? And why did he want to destroy it? Hunch thought to himself. "Someone needs to replace this forest that you keep chopping down!" but he didn't dare say a word.

Suddenly Quiz leapt off a branch and sat on Hunch's hump.

"Yuk!" said Tax, jumping back. "What's that? An enormous rat!"

Hunch peered up at the woodcutter's smirking face. Had it not been for the hump, that dragged him into a forward stoop, Hunch would have stood as tall as Tax or taller. But with the hump pressing him forward in a stoop, Tax appeared much taller than he. Tax looked down at Hunch's uplifted face and seemed to think hard for a moment, then said, "Drats! Horrid rats! Horrid Hunch. What a bunch! Ha ha, you make quite a team, it would seem! You hapless lump of horrible hump! Hey, I'm a poet and yeah, I know it!"

Tax was disappointed that there was nobody but Hunch to listen and cheer him on.

Hunch felt every cruel word. They made him feel small. And just this once, he dared to say something.

"Those trees you cut were standing long

before you were born. They would have stood long after you and I are gone. Why do you cut so many of them?"

Tax just roared with laughter.

"There are thousands of trees, and I don't ever hear them complain!"

"How can they?" asked Hunch, "They can't talk."

Tax laughed again. He was loving this.

"Of course they can't talk, you fool. They have no feelings at all. And like you they're all twisted up! See, you're not so different after all!"

Tax howled with laughter, and just for the fun of teasing Hunch, he took his axe and swung it at the nearest tree. The bark spat and the wood creaked and the trunk groaned.

Tax headed off, whistling happily.

Hunch sat down on one of the smooth stone stools below Quiz's Tree and felt the squirrel rub her soft fur against his neck. She seemed to know that he was sad. He picked up a stick that was lying on the ground. He had tears in his eyes, and he began to peel the bark off the stick, first one thread then the next. He was deep in sad thought as he split the wood into thin splinters. He sat there whittling sticks for ages. He almost forgot all about Quiz, who sat quietly nestling on his shoulder. After a long while she shifted, and Hunch startled. He knew it was her, but he looked back to take a look. Her eyes came right up to his, right up close. He could see the depths of her soul in them. Suddenly Hunch had an idea. He gathered several longer sticks and started to weave them together. He was surprised at how nimble and strong his hands were. He interlaced the sticks together. Soon he had it – a tiny chair – just the right size for Quiz. He lifted her up and put her in it. She pawed around it for a while, like a cat on a cushion, and then curled up and closed her eyes, comfortable and safe.

Hunch sat, lost in misery. And just as twilight waned into darkness, Tax came walking by. Tax was surprised to see Hunch still there, where he had mocked him hours before. He saw the chair with Quiz curled up in it, and gave it a kick. Quiz awoke with a fright, then bolted up a tree. Tax laughed. Hunch stood up and glared at him. He tightened his fists. But he knew that fighting was wrong, and Tax would beat him up anyway. How could he hope to win, with that horrid lump making him hunch? Instead he picked up the broken chair and carried it home for repair. Tax grinned. Hunch was such an easy target!

# Chapter 3
# The Feast and the Furniture

Soon afterwards school was out. The summer holidays had arrived!

Hunch was sooooo pleased! Not only had he passed his exams – this was good enough believe me. But even better, he had six glorious weeks away from school.

He was not so pleased about the summer job that he'd landed for himself – or rather that his parents had landed for him. Hunch was growing older now and his parents felt it would do him good to try his hand at working for a living.

Tax's dad had spoken to Hunch's father and said, "We will give your lad a job for the summer. He won't earn much you understand, but it will get his foot through the door. Tax tells me Hunch is good with his hands. We are soon to be holding the village dance. Hunch could help us make some decorations."

Hunch tried to warn them. Any scheme

dreamed up by Tax was bad for him. But his parents thought the job was a great idea. Hunch soon learned what Tax was up to. Tax's parents were making sure Tax had all sorts of dance lessons: he learned how to do the foxtrot and the full moon walk, even the woodcutter's chop. Tax of course wanted Hunch around for one reason. Cannon fodder. The lessons were in the same barn where the village dance was to be held, and that was where Hunch had to work.

Tax kept trying to pull Hunch into the dancing. Not to make him feel included. To show himself off. Hunch felt such a fool. If he said he did not want to dance people sniggered and thought him a coward. If he tried, the weight of his stoop made him stumble about like a giddy parrot with broken wings. Tax and the others howled with laughter.

So Hunch worked the wood the best he could. And his best was very, very good. The plan had been for Hunch to make little wooden decorations for the ball. But seeing how well Hunch worked the wood, the plan soon changed. Hunch was given long planks of timber from the trees that Tax had felled. Hunch showed spectacular skill at sawing, chiseling, hammering, nailing and polishing the wood.

Soon they moved him from the barn and into a large shop that Tax's parents owned on the high street. Out the back was a little workshop, and the first thing they had Hunch make was a sign. Carved into a large slice of tree cut down by Tax. Chiseled by Hunch's own skilful hands, the sign read: 'Tax The Axe's Furniture Shop.'

Hunch did not want to work in that shop. If only he had a friend by his side. One evening he put Quiz into her woven stick-work chair and tried to carry her into the village. But as they approached the cluster of houses and shops, she leapt out and scampered away. She did not want to be around lots of people. She did not like village noise or bustle. And Hunch did not want her to be unhappy, so he let her run away. He would see her soon enough, back by the edge of the forest. But now he would work alone.

To make the days go faster, Hunch worked busily in the workshop at the back of that little shop in the centre of the village. He crafted tables, chairs, wardrobes, candle sticks, fruit bowls, chopping boards, and even garden dragons!

Now you may be thinking, making all that furniture must take a lot of trees. And you know that Hunch loved the forest. But for every tree that Tax chopped down, Hunch planted two new saplings.

Tax sold Hunch's handmade furniture at such a handsome price in Tax The Axe's Furniture Shop that the young woodcutter had bought his family the largest house in the village. Tax knew Hunch had no head for sums. He lived in a world of riverbanks and squirrels. Tax never stopped smiling. The poorer he kept the hunchback, the richer he got himself.

One day the young woodcutter came up with a plan to make himself even richer. Why not turn the village dance into a feast? He would invite everyone in the village of course and everyone in the surrounding villages as well. He wished to show off his fine tables and chairs. When they were full of food and merry, the guests would open their purses and spend their money.

Tax called the village scribe, whose job it was to write important messages by hand. The woodcutter dictated carefully and slowly to the scribe. The scribe wrote each word speedily yet elegantly down onto long rolls of parchment. When done, the message read: 'You are invited to the village of Tax the Axe when the moon is next full. Come along for the greatest feast ever. You shall enjoy food and wine, music, dancing, and stories, with the loveliest furniture in all the land to rest upon. Everyone is invited.'

The scribe read the finished notice back to the woodcutter, who nodded thoughtfully. Then the young woodcutter said:

"One last thing to add, Scribe."

The scribe's delicate fingers danced upon the shaft of the pen, which in turn danced upon the paper and wrote exactly what the woodcutter said: "The food and wine and entertainment are free. But the furniture isn't! Sample our wares. No obligation. But bring your purses and bring 'em full, to avoid disappointment."

Tax dropped a pile of copper coins which he'd taken from Hunch's coat pocket into the scribe's hand. "Now, get busy and copy this message out one hundred times. Nail it to trees, benches, lamp posts, doors, all about the village and the towns beyond!"

Now the woodcutter's statement: 'Everyone is invited' was not quite true. For Tax had forgotten someone, without even giving him a thought. You can already guess who had slipped his mind, can't you?

You're right! That same sorry soul whose skill it was Tax hoped to profit from. After all, the sight of Horrid Hunch might scare off his customers.

Hunch first came across the message on a sign nailed to a tree beside the bridge. He sat there for a while on the riverbank. Quiz jumped nimbly about his knees as he read it. The notice said "Everyone is invited," thought Hunch. The idea of a feast was enticing! People in the village had never liked him much, but by the sounds of it people might be coming from other towns and villages as well. There would be food and stories, dancing and music! Well he could stay out of sight for the dancing. Hunch knew his parents hated large crowds, so they would not even think of going. And Quiz was scared of the people. So he would have to go alone.

Taking courage, he decided that he must swallow his fear and give it a go. The notice said the feast would be held when the moon was full. And so it was that Hunch watched earnestly each night as the moon grew from a slim slither of winking light into a blossoming globe.

On the evening of the feast Hunch put on his finest trousers and his best shirt. He pulled out a smart waistcoat he had been given one birthday but never worn – it pulled too tight across his hump, and made him look even more disfigured. But he wanted to wear his best clothes as a sign of respect. He took some scissors and cut a thin line in the waistcoat's thread, across the back just above his shoulder. This allowed it to slip more easily across his back. He brushed his hair and even added a little oil to flick his fringe out and hold it in place. He looked into the mirror and frowned. "Ugly!" he thought, "I'm all bent up like a cabbage."

This took a lot of courage. You can see now how brave he had to be.

In the village barn, with its high stone walls and tall thatched roof, a table had been set with one hundred and one chairs. Each of these chairs was different to the next. Hunch had lovingly and carefully crafted each of them with his own hands. The long tabletop gleamed with the smoothness of the carefully sawn and planed and polished wood. Every item had been created by Hunch. Wooden bowls and cups waited eagerly to be filled. Elegant candle-holders waited to be lit with the onset of night, still some hours away. A stillness of calm hung in the air. And each of the items that made up this festive table, from the wooden bowls and cups to the candle holders and the table and chairs, everything had a price tag attached. A little crass perhaps? But you must remember, after all, that the evening was Tax's idea and all he was interested in was making a healthy profit. He never gave the slightest thought to the fact that everything had been made by Hunch. It was all part of Tax The Axe's Furniture Shop.

The young woodcutter rubbed his hands together in eager anticipation. The musicians arrived, followed by the dancing girls in a bustle of giggles and frills. Then the first of the guests appeared. They arrived in such numbers that the roar of their merry voices filled the barn. The band struck up a lively jig as Tax the woodcutter stood back and watched everything with an eager eye, licking his dry lips. His heart was beating a little faster than usual. He saw every face in the village was there – well, all except one, but he barely noticed that. There were also many people he did not recognise, who had come from miles around. Tax smiled a nervous smile, how much would these festive folk spend? They were in for a fine night that they would remember. He hoped that by the time they left, the barn would stand silent and empty. Empty not just of people and food, stories and music – but also of the furniture and cups and bowls the people now used in the feast.

Tax sniffed and held up his nose as a few last stragglers arrived – a man and woman with their three children, an old gentleman with a walking stick accompanied by a small terrier dog on a lead. There were only five empty seats left at that great long table, then four, then three, then two, then one. A hundred seats filled! Tax waved his hand, and instantly as if from nowhere a small army of cooks appeared, carrying between them towering wooden platters bundled high with cheese, steaming warm bread, pies and pastries, cakes and flans. Two mighty wild boar were carried in on long poles, still sizzling from roasting on spits, snouts open as if in silent protest. Next came a team of waiters carrying Hunch's wooden serving pots piled high with fire-roasted potatoes and glazed carrots dug up this very day fresh from the fields. Corks were popped with a sound like gunfire. Wine poured in golden streams from the uncorked stems into long wooden cups made by Hunch's own hands.

Into the barn walked Hunch, in his polished boots, with his white neatly buttoned shirt and his carefully cut and threaded waistcoat (worn in a pointless attempt to hide his hump). In one hand he carried his staff, a finely crafted length of twisted hazel, that helped him carry his uncentred weight. In the other he held a small leather pouch of copper coins. After all, the posters had told everyone to bring some money along.

Hunch's eyes opened wide at the sight before him – the gleam of the candlesticks and the shine of the table, the wide wooden platters piled high with breads, cheeses, pastries, roast potatoes and delicious pies. But Hunch was only interested in one thing: finding Tax the woodcutter. As he caught his eye Hunch walked toward him. Awkwardly crossing the length of the hall he offered a hand to shake, to say well done and give his thanks for the invitation.

Tax's eyes flashed and his cheeks flushed a brilliant red as he stared hard at the hunchback.

"Get out!" he hissed.

Hunch was caught by surprise.

"But the invitation said 'Everyone is invited!'"

"That hardly means you!" spluttered Tax as he almost spat out the words, unable to contain his temper.

Hunch felt his heart sink. With all the work he had been doing for the shop, Hunch had dared to think that Tax had become his friend. Time seemed to freeze as Hunch stood there open-mouthed with one hand frozen stretched forward in friendship and the other trembling on the hilt of his staff.

The eyes of the woodcutter flashed in anger.

"This is a very important evening," he snarled. "I need these good folk who have come from near and far to be merry. I want them to buy now, and come back to purchase more later. One look at you will turn their stomachs!"

He pointed one stern finger at the door. "Out!" he roared.

# Chapter 4
# Into the Forest

Hunch felt as bad as any dog kicked by its master. He stood there, his eyes welling with tears, his mouth hanging open, in the middle of that barn full of merry music and laughter. Suddenly he felt as if everyone was laughing at him. He wished that the floor of the barn would open up and swallow him whole. How stupid he had been thinking he could attend. The woodcutter was right! He was too ugly for other people to want around.

Hunch dropped his bag of copper coins. They burst open and went rolling and spinning across the floor in all directions. For the first time since he was a very little boy, Hunch began to run. He hobbled along in a lurching stride, gripping his hazel staff for support. And once they had carried him outside the barn, those feet of his did not stop until they reached his cottage. And once at the cottage they did not stop until they had crossed the bridge over the river. There was a voice echoing in his head, his voice, at first as silent as a whisper, and then louder than drums beating:

"Oh why, why, why was I born me?"

He did not stop running until he came to the edge of the forest. And once at the edge of the forest he ran on and on, deep inside the woods, stumbling along with the soft thud thud thud of his footfall and the gentle tack, tack, tack of his hazel staff as it peglegged him along. And the loudest sound of all was the echo in his head, that now simply said, "Why me? Why me? Why me?"

Hunch did not stop running – if you can call it that, for it was more like a rolling stumble. Fuelled by a power he never thought he had, Hunch stumbled along with his heart pounding and tears streaming down his face. Even the sharp thorns and clinging vines did not manage to halt him. Hunch became aware of how thick and tall the trees were now. Their old gnarled trunks rose from the dank earth as feeble strands of waning sunlight struggled through gaps in the canopy. And only here, only now, did he finally stop.

Hunch felt the ache in his legs, and the beating of his exhausted lungs within his chest. He had run and run, as best he could with that stupid lump on his back. He felt dizzy. This was far further than he had ever come. At school he had never run, because of that hump. But this evening he had learned he could run, or sort of at least, and a greater distance than he had ever imagined possible.

Only once he recovered his breath did the boy gather his wits and look around him. He knew immediately he should never have run so far and so deep into the forest. What of the strange creatures that were said to live here in its shadowy depths? Things so strange that nobody could describe them? Looking around, all he saw was trees in every direction.

Hunch had always seen the trees as his friends, especially since he had planted so many saplings to make up for Tax's chopping. He suddenly thought of his friends the squirrels. They were always following him around whenever he was near the forest. A brief flame of hope burned in his heart. He tried to scan the uppermost branches, looking for some sign of little Quiz up there darting about. But here the trees stood too high and too thick, and there was too much shadow among the tangled branches to see anything clearly.

He stood, surrounded by the deepness of

the forbidden centre of the wild forest. Unfamiliar trees towered above him like silent sentinels. Their trunks stretching into the shadows. Hunch trembled. What if some terrible creature was lurking behind the very next trunk? He sensed the darkness thickening, and now he knew that somewhere out there, beyond the endless wall of forest, the sun was sinking low across the edge of the world. Soon it would be night.

He had better get going! He turned to head for home, but the darkness stood close around him. All he could see were more and more trees, fading into the thickening shadow. Then he spotted a short trail that might have been left by his passage through the forest. The forest floor was hard with fallen twigs and cracked earth. He could not be sure which way was back. He walked a few steps with his staff going tack, tack, tack alongside him, and then he stopped.

What if the noise of his tapping stick had disturbed some foul creature? He was out here all alone!

"God how I hate being me!" he thought with a sob. "Life is so unfair!"

Hunch took a few panicked footsteps in one direction, then he turned and went another, and then he turned again. Tears welled up in his eyes and a sore ache began to throb in his chest and his throat. He had no idea which direction he had come from. With a sense of rising terror, he admitted that he was lost.

What was he to do? Was it safer to stay still and quiet in this one place, or should he dare to try to find his way out, even if he made some noise? What would you do if this happened to you?

# Chapter 5
# The Wooden Eye

Walking as silently as he could, Hunch stumbled on as the shadows leapt from the unwelcoming trunks of the trees. Roots and burs and thorny vines reached out and snagged him. He soon ripped holes in his best trousers and tore his fine shirt but he didn't mind. He was thankful for those sturdy polished boots he had worn for the feast. The feast! He had forgotten all about it in his forlorn fear. The memory brought a sad sigh to his lips. It seemed so far away now, even though he knew he could run back there soon enough, if only he could remember the way. How long had he been running before he stopped? And where had he found the energy?

Maybe he should just make as much noise as he could, and either someone might come and save him, or some nasty critter of the forest would come and finish him off? But he did not fancy being someone's meal and so he kept walking along as silently as he could. Twigs creaked and snapped, making him flinch. This was dangerous.

He was making too much noise. After a while, as he wandered aimlessly along, he stopped worrying about the racket he was making. There was no way of stopping it. The bracken was crisp on the forest floor. Silver shafts of soft moonlight struggled through the twisted branches above.

"There is a full moon up there," Hunch thought to himself. "I wish I was out in the open."

The closeness of the trees both comforted and disturbed him. They kept him hidden from the horrible things that everyone said lurked in the forest. But the trees also gave them somewhere to hide and spy on him, ready to pounce.

All of a sudden Hunch saw it. One of the trees had a huge round wooden eye, the size of his fist, and it was staring straight at him. Hunch shivered with fright and stood stock still, eyeballing the eye that was eyeballing him. He tried hard not to blink, but the more he thought of not blinking, the more he wanted to, and then he did. When his eyes flashed open again, the wooden eye was gone, and instead there was just a twisted gnarly whorl in a tree. Hunch stayed still and staring, wondering if it had been some trick of the moonlight through the shadows. Sighing, he wandered along, right past the very spot where the tree had been staring at him.

Stumbling along in no particular direction he came to a big outcrop of boulders which sat at the bottom of a steep stone cliff. Scraggly trees poked their frail limbs out from cracks in the rocky wall, and suddenly Hunch had an idea. Maybe if he climbed this cliff he would find himself on higher ground and see past the edge of the forest. Maybe he would be lucky enough to see which way to walk to get home. Huh! Him? Lucky? When? Exactly! Luck was not his friend and never had been. Good luck was for people like Tax. The thought of the name made the hunchback scowl, and for a moment all the pain of all the years that Tax had spent taunting and mocking him flooded back. In that moment Hunch just wanted to give up on life, right there and then. To lie back and let the forest shadows and the unimaginable things that lived there do their worst to him. But Hunch had not been through so much torment – all those years of feeling alone and unwanted and ugly – to give up on himself now. He hated his hump, and what it did to him. But somewhere out there he had his parents and his best friend Quiz, and her whole dray of squirrels, and the river's lovely song, and the young forest of sapling trees he had planted. All these things he loved. He did have goodness in his life, if he thought about it: things that made his life worth living, it was as if in that moment he could hear them cheering him on, even though the woods were silent.

Hunch grabbed one of the twisted trees whose thin trunks were creeping from the steep stone wall of the cliff, and used his strength to pull himself up. The trees and the shards of cracked stone they grew from, formed a kind of staircase. Not the sort of stairs you can walk up whistling without a care in the world. This natural staircase was all pitted and twisted and topsy turvy, and grew in a thin and ragged line up the course of the steep cliff wall. But nonetheless Hunch found that with courage and with care he could begin to climb it. After what seemed like hours of pulling himself up past creaking branches and mossy outcrops of jutting stone, sheer exhaustion ground him to a halt. He was sweating and his arms and shoulders felt raw. This climb was testing a will he never thought he had. His fingers felt as if they could not grasp another branch. He sat there, on a steep fist of jutting stone, with his arms draped over a small tree that was the next step in his staircase to the sky. He had to give up. This was too much!

He sat there for a moment as droplets of

sweat rolled off him and dripped down to the forest floor. Would any nasty thing see it shine as it fell in the moonlight? Or smell him? "Humans must smell like food to the things living here," he thought. "What happens if I give up now?"

The idea of climbing back down into the dark heart of the forest made him twitch. A bundle of nerves, Hunch looked out and saw that his climb had brought him level with the highest branches of the tallest trees. The mighty trees thrust themselves up from the forest floor to drink as much sunlight as they could by day, and swim in the silver moonlight by night. But he had reached as high as they could, and there above him, above the uppermost ragged lip of the cliff, was the gorgeous round moon, washing the world in her healing silver light.

Hunch took a deep breath and using more strength than he believed he had, he continued his upward climb. Like some sort of insect, he crawled from branch to branch and from rocky foothold to rocky foothold. Slowly, ever so slowly, he crept upward towards the top of this world. And when he reached the place where the cliff suddenly gave up, Hunch carried on. With a last gasp of effort he dragged himself over the stone lip and onto flat and solid ground.

He lay there on his curved back like an upturned beetle and panted deeply. To his surprise he realised it had never felt so good to be alive. Here in the untamed forest he had accomplished something he had never thought possible. Never in his wildest dreams! He had fought against his own fears and physical exhaustion to climb that cliff in the shadowy light. Now here he was at the cliff's top. He lay there a long moment, contented and happy. For a moment, he forgot all fear. For a moment, he forgot aching limbs. For a moment, he forgot his loneliness. For a moment, he forgot his doubt and self loathing. For a moment, he forgot his hump. He forgot he was one tiny person in the middle of a terrible place, a forest of legendary horrors, inhabited by things so dreadful, that nobody could bring themselves to describe them. But he would soon remember. Very soon indeed. And once he did, that young lad lying there gazing at the happy stars – in a moment of sweet memory that would stay with him forever – I assure you that once he discovered what truly lay within that wild forest, his life would end as he knew it, and he would never be the same again.

# Chapter 6
# The Inner Circle

We all have moments in life that feel good. Hunch had not had many of them. We all have moments in life that feel terrible. Hunch had had plenty of them. And then there are those moments in life, if we are lucky, when life feels so good in that little slice of time we don't want it to end. But we know it must. Hunch wanted to lie there on that cliff top forever as the stars studded that dark sky with diamonds in the silver moonlight. Looking back, he would always return to this delicious moment. He knew he would never forget it, no matter how long – or how short – he lived.

But the night was cold, and as the joy subsided, he realised he had better get a move on. He grabbed his staff and leaned into it, pulling himself up onto his knees, then he heaved himself up until he was standing forward in a stoop. So much for conquering the world. He was Hunch the horrid hunchback again. Horrid by name, horrid by nature. Shunned by all but his own parents and a handful of squirrels.

He began his cumbersome walk across the plateau. This, like the land below, was covered in trees, save for the area of rough ground at the cliff top, where he had enjoyed his moment of triumph. He had climbed up here to try to see where his village was, but peering out all he could see were dark treetops, crested silver here and there when moonlight reflected from the canopy. There was nothing to do but climb back down the cliff, or enter the thick wedge of trees that grew across the hilltop. So he entered this new patch of forest. The trees were tall and shrouded together, just as they had been further below. Hunch was walking along, leaning as ever on his staff with each step. He was just pondering how little he had actually achieved by climbing the cliff when he found himself stepping through a line where the trees held cautiously back, forming a circle around an open clearing. I say the clearing was open, but that is not quite true.

# Chapter 7
# The White Tree

Within the circle of trees another circle had been formed. This inner circle was made from huge fallen logs all rolled loosely together, tip to tip. The logs were not really logs at all, but more like whole tree trunks turned over on their side, with no branches and no leaves. Tree trunks that had turned as white as bone, as white as death itself, all lying there in a ragged circle, waiting for something to happen.

Hunch did not like this place. And to make matters worse, there in the very middle of that scattered circle of fallen trunks, stood a single tall tree. It too was as white as bone, and it had no branches or leaves whatsoever growing from it. It was jagged at the tip, perhaps as the result of a lightening strike. It pointed at the sky like a thick boney finger.

Hunch stayed back in the safety of the trees. He stood for a while, silent, still, then when he dared, he took a step forward. Just one. Then another. Peering about him, he got to the first fallen tree that formed part of the white circle, and he stopped. He waited. He looked. He listened. He even sniffed the air, like Quiz would do checking for danger. But there was nothing to see, nothing to hear, nothing to smell. Then he walked into the circle of bone-white fallen trees. Would you have done that? Maybe you would.

He took one step, then another, his eyes scanning the dark ridge of trees that peered down on him from the shadows. The forest seemed to deepen in darkness as the young hunchback stepped awkwardly further into the open, below the dancing light of the full moon. He peered hard into the trees in every direction. He could not help feeling something had woken, something was watching him. Something very quiet. Something very still. But the trees were dark and kept their secrets. Just like if you are in a lit room at night, you cannot see out into the darkness, but someone outside in the dark could see in. Hunch could tell that someone was watching him. He could feel it.

Hunch held his staff of twisted hazel very firmly in his hand. He might have to wield it as a weapon. Hunch had never been violent. Not even against Tax when he was being bullied. But this was different. He might have to fight, just to protect his life, and that staff of twisted wood that helped him walk along was the only protection he had.

He walked now further into the circle, to get further from the line of trees. The trees had always been his friends. But now their darkness taunted him. He could not see into them. The silvery moonlight picked him out nicely for any creatures waiting to pounce.

He was walking toward the large tree in the centre. It's bone white branchless length pointed up to the nest of stars in the pitch black sky. And then Hunch saw it. There at the bottom of the tree was a dark crack. Wide enough and just high enough for him to slip inside. "The tree must be hollow," he thought. But he also thought of all the creatures that might make their home in a hollowed out tree like this one, high up on a hill surrounded by forest, far from human beings. Centipedes? Spiders? Snakes? Would you enter into a hollow below a tree like that?

What if you felt the forest all around was watching you, and all you wanted right now was to get away from those watching eyes?

With a nervous lick of his lips and a worried groan Hunch stooped onto his knees and crawled inside like a hermit crab seeking out a new shell.

It was dark inside, but not too dark. Silvery light beamed in through the crack. "But it's dark enough in here to hide all sorts of creepy crawlies!" Hunch thought to himself.

Hunch did not know whether he wanted to sweep his hands around and have a good feel of the tree's insides to find out if anything was lurking there, or to keep his hands to himself. He wrapped himself up tight and thought about it. And despite feeling so sorry for himself, here huddled up in a tree surrounded by who knows what, with a clearing outside surrounded by a forest which legend says is inhabited by dreadful, indescribable ghastly things – the very things he felt may be watching him now – despite all this and being so far from home, he fell asleep.

Hunch does not remember how long he was asleep for, but he remembers how he woke up.

RATT   TATTA   RATT   TATTA   RATT   TATTA BANG!!!

RATT   TATTA   RATT   TATTA   RATT   TATTA BANG!!!

Hunch stirred. There was a terrible racket going on outside. What could be going on to cause such a disturbance in the village? He covered his ears and tried to stay asleep. Moments later his eyes shot wide open. He wasn't in the village! He was in a clearing, deep in the forbidden forest, in the belly of a bone white tree.

RATT TATTA RATT TATTA RATT TATTA BANG!!!

RATT TATTA RATT TATTA RATT TATTA BANG!!!

Wider awake every second, Hunch sat curled up with his hands wrapped round his knees, and listened.

RATT TATTA RATT TATTA RATT TATTA BANG!!!

RATT TATTA RATT TATTA RATT TATTA BANG!!!

What was that sound? It was some sort of drumming! But what sort of drumming? And who was doing it? Hunch sat curled up inside that bone white finger of a tree for what seemed like absolutely ages, hoping the sound would stop and that whoever – or whatever – was making it would go away.

RATT TATTA RATT TATTA RATT TATTA BANG!!!

RATT TATTA RATT TATTA RATT TATTA BANG!!!

But it was useless. Whoever – or whatever – it was, had no intention of stopping, and probably even less of going away.

Hunch wanted so much to take a peek and see who, or what, it was. Would you stick your head out of that crack in the stump of that dead tree and peer around the clearing with that strange drumming going on outside? Would you?

Well Hunch did not want to. He did not think it very wise. He would get seen, most likely, and after that, things might go horribly wrong! Whatever happened next might be a very big price to pay just for seeing it. Or them.

But the longer it went on, the longer he had to sit and listen to that racket. And the more he wanted to know who – or what – was making it.

"Oh OK. I'll do it then!" he thought finally and stuck his head out through the wide crack in that bone-white tree that thrust towards the sky like a dead finger.

RATT TATTA RATT TATTA RA...

Suddenly the drumming stopped, just as Hunch saw who was doing it. He was looking at them. For it was not an it. It was a them. More than one, many more.

They were sat there on those fallen tree trunks around the edge of the clearing. Each of them carried bones as drumsticks. Bones from fish. Bones from birds. Even bones from deer, bones from badgers and – Hunch thought with a lump in his throat – bones from squirrels. There were not any human bones there, at least Hunch did not think so, but he could not be sure.

They sat and beat the bones against the large white fallen tree-trunks upon which they were sitting. But apart from that it was very hard, if not impossible, to describe them.

You see although there were perhaps a hundred of them or more, sat all crowded together around the fallen trees that circled the clearing, no two of them were exactly the same. They were all the same colour, a sort of rather unpleasant snot green. Eeeewwww... but worse than that, they were the same shape as bogeys too, and what shape is a bogey? Not the sort of bogey you just pick out of your nose and it sort of sits there in a slimy little lump of goo on the unhappy tip of your finger. No not like that at all! They were more the shape of a bogey that you have pulled around a bit in your fingers, ferrying it this way and that, and stretched in different directions, then added eyes in the oddest of places, legs in the oddest of places, arms in the oddest of places and so on. Now what shape is that? It's hard to say, especially when each and every one of them is completely different to the next.

Some have their fingers where you have your nose. And some have their nose where you have your toes. Some have their toes where you have your tongue, and some have their tongues where you have your legs. Some have their legs where you have your neck. And some don't. Some have ten necks, and some have no neck at all. Some have one head, just like you, but then others have two. Or three heads, or ten. Some their heads bubble up like welts from tiny spots till they are more like balloons, with eyes and noses, mouths and maybe arms or legs growing from them. Then the heads pop like acne, before growing back again.

Given time, you can describe how most creatures look. But not this mob. That is why we just call them Things – because they are too hard to describe. No two of these Things looked the same.

And there, sitting on the largest trunk, right opposite the crack in the tree where Hunch had stuck out his head, was their King.

# Chapter 8
# The King Of The Things

Many have asked, "What does The King Of The Things look like?" Well I shall try my best, but you see it really is quite impossible. You see he just kept on shifting. I don' t mean shifting like you might shift, you know, by twitching your foot or adjusting your back or tapping your fingers. No no! The King Of The Things, he really shifted. For example your torso as you may know is that part of your body with your head at the top, with arms either side, and two legs probably sprouting out from the bottom. When Hunch first glimpsed him, the Thing King's torso was attached to four legs and no arms but six huge eyes bobbing around like corks. He looked something like an enormous brain, all crinkly and round, with three huge round nostrils, dripping yellow wax onto the forest floor. But then suddenly he didn't look like that at all, but instead he looked rather like a dangerously beautiful kind of man-eating flower, in a ghastly sort of way. Then quick as a flash he grew what looked like duck's feet, except they were growing from the place where his ears would have been, if it was you. One moment he had a hundred eyes all blinking along the length of twelve arms. Eye lashes fluttered and glowed bright as butterfly wings as he waved those arms about. And what looked like a tiger's tail appeared on the top of his head, except his head was now growing where you have your belly. And a dandelion in full bloom sprouted where you would have a face, until it blew off in a tiny storm of white seeds like dandelions do in a gust of wind. He had claws where you have your knees, and then no claws at all. Suddenly he had eight arms, really strong ones corded with muscle. Sharp pointed turrets of bone, something like rhinoceros horns, sprouted their way along each arm. His arms grew out from the sides of his legs. But then everything changed again. Yes, what exactly did the King Of The Things look like? You tell me? In fact if you happen to be brave enough, we'll leave a whole blank page at the end of this book for you to write it down, if you dare, or draw a picture, or maybe even both.

Poor Hunch found The King Of The Things most unpleasant and horrifying to look at. He was suddenly rather pleased his parents were not there, for fear of having to carry them all the way back through the forest after they had fainted.

Hunch pulled himself back into the hole below the tree. He thought it would be better to stay hiding in there throughout the night. But in a voice that sounded something like an elephant's trumpet mixed with a lion's roar, (with a little bit of meerkat bark thrown in), The King Of The Things said:

"Ah ha, Samesey, don't you hide away! We see you in there! Now come out and show yourself, or we may have to eat you for being so rude!"

Hunch felt like pretending he had not heard, or that he thought the King was speaking to someone else. After all he was not called 'Samesie'! But he knew the King Of The Things was talking to him.

Hunch peered at the strange gathering of Things that yammered and howled, growled and garumbled upon the rough circle of fallen trunks around him. Hunch guessed they would eat him as soon as they could, if only their King allowed it. Some of the Things had sharp curved claws that gleamed in the moonlight, others had enormous pincers, or poison dripping from their wings. Hunch decided he had better do exactly as he was told. So he pulled himself right out from the tree, dragging his walking staff behind him. He stood there wide-eyed and quaking, as he beheld the terrible King Of The Things right there in front of him.

"Ha ha!" roared the King in merry mirth and all the Things around the circle echoed him:

"Ha ha!" they called.

Hunch wished his knees would stop knocking from the sheer fright of the sight of them.

"You Samesies make me laugh! No imagination! None!" the king roared.

"None! None!" hissed and haloobered the others.

The hunchback quivered. He had better be polite. He bent himself as low as he could and did a little bow.

The King's nose spread wide in a large smile, his nostrils brimming with fangs.

"Now Samesie, what's your question? Every Samesie has one!"

And with that the King Of The Things stuck one long tongue out from his enormous toothed nose, which happened in that moment to be the whole of his bloated body, and licked all three nostrils. All the Things followed suit, even though some of them had more tongues, or less, or longer, or shorter, and in different places to that of the King himself. A few of them shook or rattled the bones they had been using as drumsticks, and Hunch wondered if he was quite sure none of those bones were human.

A question! The poor hunchback could not think of one! What do you ask a King of terrible Things high up on his hill in the middle of a forest, all alone, under the light of a full moon, without being eaten? Hunch's brain whirred and squeezed, juicing one tiny drop of imagination out of his terror frozen mind.

"Ah, w, w, well your Majesty, why do you call me Samesie?"

At that, half the Things fell backwards off their logs laughing, while the other half fell forward, and laughed all the more. They tumbled about, baffooing and chaboobeling merrily. The King himself floated up in the air using tiny weeny rows of wings that now grew from his tongue, and grinned broadly with his elbows.

"Why Samesie? For that is what you are! You Samesies that live in your barns and cottages, out in your villages and towns, you are all the same! One head on top. Two ears either side, two eyes out front above one nose, above one mouth, above one chin! One neck above one chest, two shoulders and an arm attached each side! One elbow in the middle, hands at the end, four fingers and one thumb. Two legs, two knees, two feet, ten toes, all down the bottom ordered and accounted for! I say, you must all like it! You all do it! You are all the same!"

The King Of The Things suddenly lowered gently onto his log and turned into a shivering cluster of feathers, with sharp spikes like a porcupine sticking through.

"Nothing wrong with being the same!" The King Of The Things said: "And nothing wrong with being different. Everyone is different to us, even we are! Ha ha! There is no better or worse. Just different. You see? But how could you? You're a Samesie!"

# Chapter 9
# Samesie

Now as you might imagine, nobody had ever called Hunch the same before. He had spent his whole life being bullied because he was different! Perhaps you would not like it much if a strange Thing on top of a mountain told you that you were a Samesie, but Hunch liked it. He liked it a lot. And all of a sudden he liked that Thing King too! He was so happy for a moment he forgot to be frightened anymore, and he simply said: "Why thank you, your Majesty!"

To that the King Of The Things and all his minions around him fell about laughing and chaborteling some more. Hunch just stood there smiling, and suddenly began laughing with them. He never would have laughed at them, for that's quite a different and far more dangerous thing. When the hoots and howls and warbles and wallaboos of laughter had subsided, the King said, "Drummers, prepare yourselves. Samesie, dance!"

Hunch dropped his smile. Dance? He

couldn't dance. Everyone in his village knew that. The hump on his back kept him off balance, and the walking stick got in his way. Tax laughed at him a lot, but never louder than when Hunch tried to dance. He could not get his feet right, or his arms, or his back, and this all threw his tempo right out. He knew it. And now here he stood in a circle of unimaginable creatures, and of everything their leader could have asked of him, the Thing King had demanded to watch him dance. Oh, why was luck never on his side?

"Dance!" roared the King. He had ten long fleshy stems growing out of his head, with a large rolling eyeball blinking red at the end of each one.

RATT TATTA RATT TATTA RATT TATTA BANG!!!

RATT TATTA RATT TATTA RATT TATTA BANG!!!

The Things beat those bones upon the dead white tree trunks where they sat, and Hunch began. He used his twisted hazel staff for support. He had to. He tapped his feet, he jumped a little this way and that. He bobbed up and down in a giddy lurch. He threw his hands one way, then the other, and he tried his best to smile.

"Stop the drumming!" shouted the King Of The Things. And the drumming stopped. All the Things sat in that circle quieter than a hiding mouse. They waited. Hunch waited. Was this the moment they would eat him?

"That was brilliant!" exclaimed The King Of The Things. "We shall have you back tomorrow!"

"Tomorrow?" gulped Hunch, hearing his own voice squeak.

"Yes tomorrow!" laughed the King. "We Things only come and drum when the moon is full. One night waxing full, that's tonight! One night waning full, that's tomorrow! "

Then the Thing King's many tentacled eyes all twisted together and grew into one as he said, "You will come back tomorrow, won't you?"

Hunch liked the King a little more than upon first sight, as you know, but still, he was petrified. If he could leave this place alive he never planned to come back.

The King Of The Things must have sensed this for that one enormous eye narrowed as he said, "I tell you what little Samesie. I shall give you a gift. Half now, half later when you return."

With that he reached out with one long leg and opened up a large fold of wrinkled skin that for a moment sat there hidden at the side of his head. A dark hole opened up below it, belching green steam. With his noses at the end of his toeses he reached into that hole and squished and squelched and squalooed around. Then with a pop and a puff he pulled out a leather pouch, all dripping with snot green slime.

"Here you go little Samesie. We like you. Take this!" he said, and held the bag forward toward the hunchback.

Would you have picked up that belching parcel of slithery gunge and taken it out of the King's nostril hands?

Hunch did not dare insult the King. The bag was about the size of a football. He reached for it. Its heaviness took him by surprise and he almost dropped it. The slime seemed very sticky. Yeek. It caught on his hand and started trickling down his arms.

"Open it! Open It!" said the King Of The Things.

RATT TATTA BANG

The drummers' hands and feet and claws and paws and feathers and tails danced, bone on wood.

Hunch did as he was told. The bag had a length of leather twine around the top and it was tied very tight. Hunch wriggled his fingers in and shuffled them about. The pouch opened and belched green clouds of mist.

Eeewwwwwwwwwwww! And there inside the bag...

Hunch's eyes almost popped out of their sockets. He had not expected this! This was wilder than he could ever have imagined. Not him. Not Hunch. Holding this.

The bag was so heavy because it was full of gold. Big coins. Little coins. Thick coins and thin coins. All a-gleaming. All a-glimmering. All gold. All his?

Hunch stared up at the Thing King. Right now he was a sort of huge eagle butterfly, with whiskers and a long feathery tail.

"Is this...?" asked Hunch, but before he could finish his tongue seemed to stick in his mouth with surprise. He could not speak.

"For you!" said the King Of The Things. "For your excellent dancing. That is half. Yes half. Come back tomorrow, entertain us. And there shall be more."

Hunch just nodded. He did not know what to say. "Thank you!" would have suited just fine, but his head was too amazed to give him the words.

"Now go!" said the King Of The Things.

"We Things have other business to attend to! Go home! And we shall expect you for more dancing tomorrow!"

Hunch was confused. Standing there weighed down with his hump on his back, and the bag of gold in his arms. Home? He did not know the way. He found his voice and asked.

All the Things pointed. Straight toward Hunch's village, where the Samesies lived. Pointing with their fingers. Pointing with their noses. Pointing with their eyebrows, or the tips of their toeses.

The King Of The Things opened up that flap again. This time it was under one very green and goey armpit.

"Here's a map!" he said.

Slime Goo drip, drip, drip.

Hunch took the soggy map. He could hardly believe it. They were letting him go! He was not going to be eaten! And he was rich!

"Thank you your Majesty!" he said, at last finding his voice. And he turned to leave in the direction the Things were pointing, with the map under one arm, and his pouch of gold in the other. He took a step, then another. It was difficult balancing his staff, with his hands so full. He reached the edge of the clearing. One more step and he would be gone from the clearing and back in the forest, on his way back home.

"Stop!" called the King Of The Things.

Would you have stopped? Hunch did think of running into the shadows. But he knew the forest stretched out far ahead of him, and did not much like the idea of all those strange and terrible indescribable Things leaping and climbing and swooping and burrowing through the forest after him.

"Yes, your Majesty?" asked Hunch, turning with a little bow, his knees knocking and his hands all a-tremble. Was he not going to escape with his life, let alone his gold, after all? In that moment the gold did not even matter. All he wanted was his life.

The King Of The Things glared at him with the tips of his squinting ears. "How do I know you will come back? Yes – if you do, you get more gold. But now you have enough gold to make you rich for your whole life long in the world of Samesies. You Samesies are all the same on the outside, but you are different on the inside. Some of you are greedy, and can never be happy because you want more, more, more. That Samesie would come back. But some of you are grateful for what you have, and even enjoy sharing it around. That

Samesie is often very happy already, and might not return to give another dance!"

The King Of The Things frowned with his pointed nose and said: "What kind are you? Samesies are all the same on the outside. But on the inside, they are different – some are better, some are worse. Courage and fear, kindness and greed. What kind are you?"

Hunch knew which kind he was. He would be more than happy with the gold he had in this pouch. It was more than he could have ever hoped for.

The King Of The Things looked stern and flapped a pair of large humming wings that had suddenly sprouted from his arms.

"I want to be sure. Will you come back tomorrow? I must take something from you which is part of you, which you really want, which will bring you back!"

Hunch trembled and said, "Your Majesty! I have nothing but the clothes I wear, my walking staff, and this gold you have so kindly given me! Apart from that there is nothing to take. I am a humble hunchback!"

"Ah ha!" roared the King. "That's what I shall take then. Only a borrow, you understand. Come and dance tomorrow below the full moon, and you shall have it back, and another bag of gold!"

With that The King Of The Things reached forward with the suction on those twitching nostril toes. And with a squelch and a squimble the King lifted that hump right off Hunch's back!

Hunch gasped. He had felt something, but what was it? His mind reeled. It couldn't be? He twisted round and patted himself on the shoulder. The hump was gone! There it was, already dripping green goo, lifted up high in a sharp talon from the snaking arm of The King Of The Things. And quick as a wink the King opened that flap of skin that was now behind one knee, and shoved the hump deep inside.

"The map will take you home, and bring you back! Go well hunchback. Go well!"

Hunch left that twisted hazel staff as a gift for the Things. It had no purpose for him now. He wasn't a hunchback anymore!

Hunch could have sworn all those Things sat in that circle of dead fallen trunks were waving at him. Hunch waved back as he set off toward home. He was standing tall, taller than he had ever stood before. He felt a new person. Such a weight lifted from him. The only weight he carried now was that pouch full of gold coins.

As he set off through that fearsome forest, he even began to whistle. He had met the dreaded unthinkable Things that lived in the wood, and they had not been half so bad on the inside, as they were on the outside. Why he would even call them his friends. Soon the soft silvery light of dawn crept into the sky and cast frail fingers of light among the branches. Birds began to twitter and whistle, and Hunch whistled too. And as he walked along, he found that the map soon led him onward through the forest perhaps faster than he might have asked for, so lovely it was there among the trees. Golden beams of sunshine began to splash through the trees. Hunch sat himself down for a moment and before he knew it, there in the blanket of sunshine, he dozed off to sleep.

He had not been asleep for long, he knew it, for still the shadows of the trees cast long fingers across the forest floor, as they do at sunrise and sunset. A gentle breeze had woken him up. He stood up and then gasped. The map had blown away! He searched for it this way and that. Which way was the wind blowing? He could feel it coming at him through the trees, and watched the leaves bend gently to the breeze's will. He stood tall on tiptoes and peered through the trees but he couldn't see the village. A new panic entered his heart. Was he to stay lost after all? He was no longer scared of the mysterious nameless things that lived in the wood. But still other creatures lived here. Wolves, bears, snakes. With each passing moment he wondered if he was walking the wrong way? Back to the Things? Or somewhere altogether different, there in the vast wild wood? The creatures of the forest gave startled calls all around him.

Suddenly there was a flash of something dark up there in the uppermost branches. A shadow leapt through the trees across his path. Hunch almost screeched in fright. He took a startled step backwards, raising his arms to protect himself. He felt small claws leap onto his back. Hunch flinched, but only for a moment. Then he laughed. Quiz's face appeared as she leant across to rub his nose with hers. Her eyes had widened with surprise. Where was his hump?

But she had another surprise for him. There held firmly in the tight roll of her bushy tail was the map. His friend had saved him. Were they near the forest edge after all?

Hunch thought Quiz might simply leap through the trees and ask him to follow her, as she had so many times before, when he had never dared enter the forest. But this time she just sat there balancing on his shoulder. Hunch consulted the map and soon the pair were travelling along together, as Hunch told Quiz all he had seen and done. It was not long before the gaps between the trees began to widen. The treetops danced with small shadows, and the other squirrels were all about. At last, Hunch and Quiz stepped out beyond the very edge of the wood, and there were the fields that led to the bridge and home.

"Come on Quiz. Will you be extra brave with me this morning? Come with me to my cottage? Not into the town, we don't need that place anymore. You knew it all along, didn't you little friend? Let's go. We have an adventure to begin!"

With that, Hunch headed for the cottage. Quiz balanced on his now much smaller shoulder and she wrapped her bushy tail round his neck like a soft scarf.

# Chapter 10
# Tax The Terrible

It was early and everyone was sleeping. One lone figure was walking slowly toward the forest, with an axe swung across his shoulder. Tax saw Hunch coming toward him from a distance, and grinned. Tax hid in the bushes at the edge of the forest. He dared not go too deep, as you know, for fear of the terrible unmentionable Things that no one can describe, which rumour has it live there. But behind a large tree he stood, and waited till Hunch walked by, then leapt out with a scream "Ah ha!"

But it was Tax who got the fright. Hunch wasn't hunching anymore. Hunch stood taller than him, and was there smiling down.

"Hunch?" said Tax, a startled look on his face.

Quiz turned her tail and flicked the woodcutter across the nose.

Tax saw Hunch standing straight and tall. He saw the map and the heavy looking pouch. "What have you got there my friend?" he asked, his eyebrows raised in surprise.

Hunch told Tax everything. About running off into the forest. Getting lost. Climbing the cliff. Finding the clearing and the circle of death white trunks. The tall tree with a hollow inside. Falling asleep. Waking to the sound of drumming. Meeting the King Of The Things. Being asked to dance. Given a bag of gold. And the promise of more if he returned.

Tax's eyes narrowed. He licked his lips. He waved Hunch goodbye and walked off to chop some trees. Or pretended too. As soon as Hunch turned a bend in the river, Tax carefully followed him. Tax watched as Hunch entered his cottage. He crept up outside. Inside he heard Hunch telling his parents all that had happened. Then Hunch said, "Mother, Father. I wish to take us all off for an adventure!"

Tax took a peek through the open window and saw the map sat right there on the table. Where was the gold? He could not see. His hand whipped inside then out again. And when Hunch sat down with Quiz and his family for breakfast, they noticed the map had gone. No worry. They had enough gold and were grateful for it. And with happy hearts they disappeared into another story.

That evening Tax gathered up all of his courage. With his trusty axe in one hand and the map in the other, he entered the forest. With a beating heart he followed the map, carefully. He never had to climb the cliff, but instead he walked along a straight and hidden pathway, with the map to guide him. It took him a long time, and the sounds and shadows startled him and made his stomach turn. But he kept thinking of that second bag of gold the stupid King had promised Hunch. A bag of gold just for a dance! What a fool!

Soon enough he came to the clearing. There were the bone white fallen trunks, all laid out in a circle. There was the tall dead tree, with the hollow inside. Tax climbed in and waited. He waited so long he fell asleep and dreamt of spiders climbing all over him. He gave a little cry of fear, and then he heard it.

RATT TATTA RATT TATTA RATT TATTA BANG!!!

RATT TATTA RATT TATTA RATT TATTA BANG!!!

The King Of The Things saw Tax's head appear from the crack in the tree's hollow.

"Aha! Samesie! You have returned!"

"He is as stupid as he is ugly!" thought

Tax. His knees knocked and a big ball of sick rose from his gut into his mouth, but he held it back, and swallowed. "Why he thinks I am that ugly hunchback!" he thought to himself.

"Welcome back!" said the King.

Tax trembled terrifically as he watched the King's large single eye turn into twelve fingers that twitched at the end of a long winding nose.

RATT TATTA RATT TATTA RATT TATTA BANG!!!

RATT TATTA RATT TATTA RATT TATTA BANG!!!

"Now dance!"

Tax almost smiled. He would show this King a thing or two. He put down his axe and began a slow waltz, all there on his own. He knew the steps so well. He then gathered speed, slipping into a quick foxtrot.

"Stop the drumming!" shouted the King Of The Things.

And the drumming stopped. All the Things sat in that circle quieter than a mouse. They waited. Tax waited. Suddenly he was sure they were about to eat him. A little warm trickle crept down his leg.

"That was ridiculous!" exclaimed The King Of The Things. "Dance as you did yesterday!"

Tax flinched. "This King cannot be serious," he thought. "Or Hunch must have lied! How could the King like Hunch's dance so much he paid for it with gold? Anyone and everyone knows Hunch can't dance, and I'm brilliant!"

RATT TATTA RATT TATTA RATT TATTA BANG!!!

RATT TATTA RATT TATTA RATT TATTA BANG!!!

Of course Tax had no idea how the hunchback had danced. He swung up his arms and did a high pirouette. He shook his tail, did the Chop and he looped and swayed and full-moon walked, but all to no avail. As he stared at the King Of The Things, some enormous eyeballs he had growing on the ends of his elbows began to turn red with fury. All the Things began oozing and twitching, grafforing and damrumbling on their fallen bone branches. A gentle roar of hullabaloos and bafungerambles rose into the air.

Tax danced the Hog's back, and even turned a cartwheel.

"Stop the drumming!" The King Of The Things scowled from behind a set of sharp fangs that sprouted from every inch of his body. But Tax did not wait to hear any more. He grabbed his axe from the floor and raised it, blubbering like a tiny child. A long crab claw shot out from the King's bellybutton and gripped the handle.

Tax could not throw or strike. He fell to his knees and began to sob. "Why are you picking on me!" he howled.

"Are you trying to have a laugh?" roared the King. "I am surprised and disappointed in you. Yesterday you were so gracious. Today you are a fool. I am the King Of The Things! You Samesies lack many things, especially the abilities of Thing King. You see?"

"Huh?" said the woodcutter, with tears flooding from his eyes.

"Say it slowly with that Samesie mouth of yours, there with two lips, right over your chin, right under your nose! Thing King! Thing King! Some of you Samesies are better at it than others. Thing King! Before you speak or act! Say it slowly!" said the King Of The Things as a long tongue rolled from underneath his armpit.

Tax began, scratching his head.

"Thing King? Thing King? Oh... thinking!"

The King Of The Things suddenly became a ball of green fur surrounded by a thousand blinking eyes.

"You judge others by how they look on the

outside, or how much gold they hold, rather than what is inside their hearts. There is no better or worse on the outside. Just different. It's the inside that counts! Now, it's time for you to go. But before you do, what's your question. Every Samesie has one!"

Tax was not used to being bossed around. He did the opposite of what The King Of The Things was telling him. He did not think at all.

Tax was used to getting his own way far too often.

He stood up and said, "Leave? Not yet! I demand my gold! I want what's mine!"

Do you think that brave? Saying it to the King Of The Things surrounded by his minions in the clearing on that hill took a little something, to be sure. But bravery is not bravery if it's just plain foolish. For a start there was no truth in it. How could Tax think it was his gold? No one had ever promised it to him! It had been promised to Hunch only if Hunch returned. But Tax had stolen the map, and come in his place. Of course Tax's question was not a question at all. Tax had to learn to listen more than he spoke. After all, that's why he had been given two ears and one mouth.

"You are right!" said the King Of The Things.

"I do have something that is yours!"

He stretched out a long gooey tongue dripping with green spit and used it to flip up the fold of skin. It formed a little gasping slit right under one of his chins. Green mist slipped down to his belly in a ball of rolling slime.

Tax smiled. He had won! He had shown The King Of The Things his rightful place. "Ha ha. Good life here I come!" he thought and rubbed his hands together. "I wonder how many bags of gold this disgusting Thing holds inside his body? I want to have them all!"

The King Of The Things pulled a spongy pouch from his belching navel. Tax reached out his hands. He twitched his nose. This parcel looked disgusting. Big and heavy, dripping gunge onto the forest floor. The King Of The Things held it high over Tax's head, then said:

"Here you go! You take it back. Keep it. Even if you can't dance!"

"Stupid King!" thought Tax.

Then, looking up, Tax recognised the shape of that dripping lump. His eyelids peeled open with terror.

"No!" he cried and turned to flee.

But The King Of The Things did not intend to put the horrid parcel in Tax's hands. He hovered it for a second, then just as Tax began to run, he slipped it onto Tax's back, where it stuck firmer than any glue, never to be removed again.

Tax felt the weight of it. It made him hunch forward. He fell onto his hands with a gasp. And right there, on the ground beside him, was Hunch's old twisted hazel staff. With a groan Tax used it to lift himself to standing. Something about the weight the King Of The Things had put across his shoulder, made him bend forward in a stoop. Tax trembled and he begged:

"Take it off. Take it off!"

With a gasp of horror he realised he could not stand up straight, no matter how hard he tried.

So this is really a story about how a little village once lost its hunchback, but soon found another. And this new one – unlike Hunch – really was rather horrid, don't you think? Because it's what's inside that counts.

Tax The Terrific soon gained a new name. Tax The Terrible. But that's a tale for another time.

To this day the village is still surrounded by fields, and the fields are indeed still surrounded by forest. For Tax never swung his axe again, his bent back would not allow it.

This story took place once upon a time, in a place not so far away. If you should ever go walking deep into a forest, and find yourself in a wide circle of trees, with fallen stumps all around, with a tall tree in the centre, pointing at the sky like a white boney finger, take a look and check if there's a hollow at the bottom. And if there is, decide whether you want to sit inside.

The author says:

"Would you like to try to draw the best ever picture of the King of the Things? We've left a big space here on this page for you..."

## Author's dedication:

'To my four teenage children: Sage, Iris, Maia, and Tamsyn. May the child within you always be aware to wonder.'

Adrian Beckingham, (A.K.A. The Man from Story Mountain) is a leading story-teller who has spun magical tales at the British Museum, Glastonbury Festival and venues across the globe. An active advocate for the power of story to transform and heal, Adrian is well known for his work using stories to improve mental health in community care arenas. He was also founding chairman of The Siddhartha Foundation, a charity establishing a residential school for Himalayan orphans in Kathmandu city.